Hansel and Gretel

Adapted by Larry Carney
Illustrated by Traci Parrish

PC Multimedia Entertainment
TREASURES, INC.

Published by

PC Multimedia Entertainment
TREASURES, INC.

2765 Metamora Road, Oxford, Michigan 48371 USA

Hansel and Gretel

Adapted by Larry Carney
Illustrated by Traci Parrish
Audio CD Reading Performed by Kara Kimmer
Songs Written by Larry Carney
Songs Produced and Performed by D. B. Harris

ISBN 1-60072-030-7

First Published 2007

Made in China.

Once upon a time, in a small cottage in the forest, there lived a poor woodsman and his loving wife along with their two adoring children—a little boy named Hansel and a little girl named Gretel.

Every day the woodsman would go off into the woods to cut down trees to sell. His wife would tend to their small vegetable garden. Hansel and Gretel would often pick wild berries. Despite all this hard work, there was rarely enough food for them to eat.

One summer things became very bad for the family. No one was buying the trees the woodsman was cutting down and the garden produced only a small amount of food. Soon, all the family had left to eat was a single loaf of stale bread.

One night, after a small supper, Hansel and Gretel lay in their beds and listened as their parents talked. "Oh, our poor children, I don't like to see them so hungry," said the woodsman. His wife put a hand on his arm and said, "Don't worry dear. Even though we are poor and hungry, we still have each other. This is the most important thing."

Gretel was sad to hear her parents worry
so. "Hansel," she whispered as she sat up
in bed, "I've been thinking—we should help
Mother and Father and bring food to the
table." Hansel whispered back, "How can
we do that?" "We'll go out in the woods to
look for food. I'm sure there are wild vegetables
there and mushrooms, too!"

"Oh, no," said Hansel. "Mother and Father have told us to never go off into the forest alone. We could get lost." Gretel shook her head, "We won't get lost—I'll make sure." She laid back down and smiled. "Oh, just think of all the wonderful food we'll find!"

Very early the next morning, Hansel and
Gretel tip-toed toward the door. As she walked
past the table, Gretel took the loaf of stale bread.
"If we leave a trail of bread crumbs, we won't
get lost," she said. With this, Hansel and Gretel
quietly walked outside.

TURN PAGE

Hansel didn't like the idea of taking the last
bit of food the family had, but Gretel told him,
"No one is going to miss this stale old bread
when they see all the food we're going to bring
back!" Hansel and Gretel went into the woods.
They walked on and on, and with every few
steps, Gretel would drop a bread crumb on the
trail to mark their way.

For several hours Hansel and Gretel walked.
Deeper and deeper into the forest they went.
As they made their way, they looked for wild
vegetables and mushrooms, but couldn't find
a single thing to eat. They were getting a little
tired, and when they came to a clearing, they
decided to rest.

Hansel looked at the loaf of bread, which had become very small, and said, "I wish we had saved some of that bread." Gretel said sadly, "I'm sorry Hansel. I really thought that we could find some food in the woods." Hansel looked at his sister, "Can we go home now? I'm getting tired." Gretel nodded.

Hansel and Gretel walked for a ways before
they realized that the bread crumbs were gone.
Hansel looked up and pointed at three strange
birds that were perched overhead. "Oh no!
Those birds must have eaten the bread crumbs!
We're lost!" Gretel put her arm around her
brother and said, "Don't worry Hansel. I
remember the way home." TURN PAGE

11

Hansel and Gretel had walked for a short
time when Hansel said tearfully, "Gretel, I
think we're going the wrong way." It was
starting to get dark outside, and they were
both getting worried about having to spend
the night in the forest.

Hansel and Gretel continued through the woods. Suddenly, the most wonderful smell drifted toward them. It was a fresh, warm, chocolate, sugar, candy smell that tickled their noses and made their hungry stomachs growl.

TURN PAGE

They followed this wonderful smell into a clearing and they couldn't believe what they saw—a house made out of gingerbread! With gingerbread walls, a frosted roof, sugar wafer windows and lollipop flowers growing all around, it was the sweetest house they had ever seen! Hansel and Gretel ran up the sugar cube sidewalk and stared in disbelief at the delicious house.

Hansel and Gretel were so hungry that they couldn't help but take a little bite out of the side of the house. It tasted so good that soon they were eating great big handfuls of the house. They both had happy smiles on their faces when they suddenly heard a soft voice say, "Nibble, nibble, nibble…who's that eating up my house?"

The door of the gingerbread house slowly opened. A little old woman looked down at them and smiled. "Oh, what have we here?" she asked. Hansel and Gretel stopped chewing and looked at her with wide eyes. The old woman waved her hand and said, "Don't worry little ones. There's no harm done."

The old woman looked at the children and said, "You poor things. You look like you haven't eaten in a week!" She told Hansel and Gretel to come inside her house. She sat them at a table and said, "I'll fix a proper meal for you." And she began cooking at the stove.

"We're sorry for eating your house ma'am," said Gretel. "Oh, don't worry about that," answered the old woman as she brought two plates to the table and set them in front of Hansel and Gretel. "Oh, I am so happy that I can have two children for dinner," the old woman said as she watched the children eat. "You both can sleep here until morning. Tomorrow I will take you home."

The next morning when Gretel woke up she
called to Hansel, but he didn't answer. Gretel
searched around the house for him. To her
surprise, she found him in a corner, locked
inside a large cage. As she walked toward him,
she heard a cruel voice say, "So, you're awake
at last you lazy creature!" Gretel turned around
to see the old woman standing there, now
transformed into an ugly witch.

19

"What's the matter? Haven't you ever seen a witch before?" she cackled. Gretel took a step back. "You've fallen for my gingerbread trap!" the witch said as she rubbed her hands together. She leaned closer to Gretel. "You see, I love children…especially when they're cooked!" The witch cackled again. "Tonight, I am going to have Hansel for dinner!"

As the frightened Hansel watched from inside
the cage, the witch stomped her foot at Gretel
and said, "Now don't just stand there! Get busy!
Light a fire in the oven!" Gretel shook her head
and said, "My parents don't allow me to play
with fire." The witch pointed at the stove and
said, "Well your parents aren't here! Do as I say
and start a fire!"

TURN PAGE

Gretel opened the oven door slowly, pretending not to know what to do. The witch shouted, "Hurry up you little brat!" Gretel stared back at the witch and said, "I don't know how to start a fire."

"What!? Are you a fool? Stand aside, I'll show you how it's done!" The witch moved to the oven and leaned inside. As she did, Gretel quickly pushed the witch into the oven with all her might. With the witch jammed tightly in the oven, Gretel closed the door.

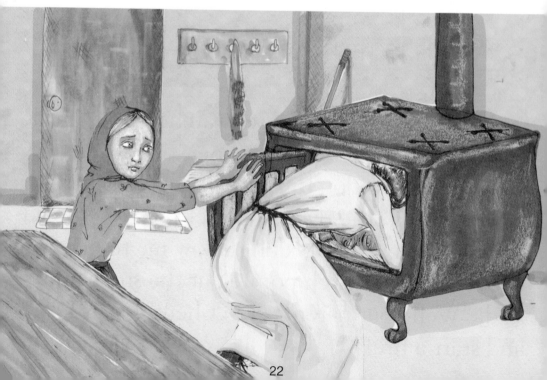

As the witch shouted to be let out of the oven, Gretel let Hansel out of the cage. They quickly walked to the door and went outside. Once outside, they heard voices calling, "Hansel! Gretel! Where are you!?" It was their parents! They had spent all day and night searching for their missing children. Hansel and Gretel ran with relief into the arms of their mother and father.

TURN PAGE

They all went home together. Before returning, the woodsman took a huge piece of the gingerbread house, which they ate for dinner that night. And the woodsman, his wife, Hansel, and Gretel all lived, through good times and bad times, very happily ever after.

Collect Them ALL!

Goldilocks and the
Three Bears

Hansel and Gretel

Little Red
Riding Hood

The Gingerbread
Man

The Little Mermaid

The Three
Little Pigs

The Ugly Duckling

Cinderella

Plus Many More

See them all and much more at
www.FairyTalePop.com

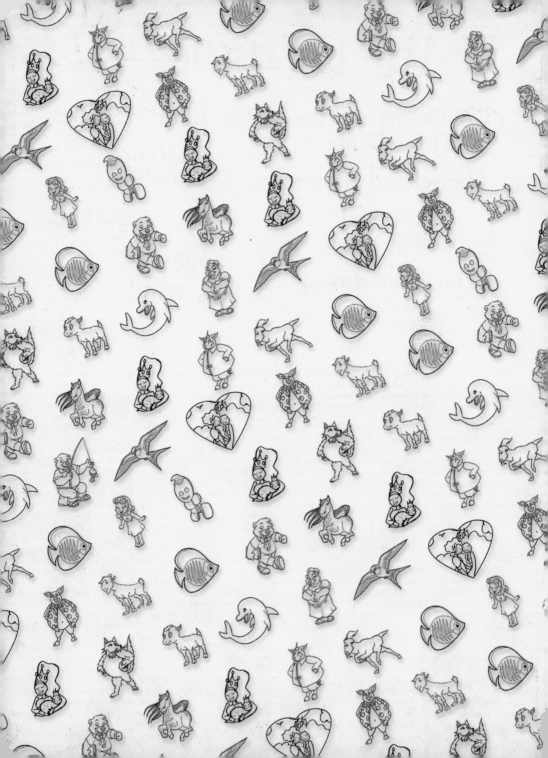